Trainer's Mini Exploration Guide

Trainer's Mini Exploration Guide

INSIGHT
EDITIONS

San Rafael · Los Angeles · London

CONTENTS

A World Full of Pokémon!

Thanks to the hard work of Pokémon Professors, more than 800 Pokémon have been discovered so far. Each Pokémon species has its own unique Evolution chain, personality, and of course, battle advantages. As a Trainer, finding the right Pokémon partners is about much more than stats! To be a top Trainer, one must not just catch Pokémon, but also become one with their Pokémon pals. This mini-guide gives you a close look at some of the wonderful Pokémon found across the regions.

PIKACHU *#025*

Ash's Pikachu is Ash's best friend! It does not like to travel in its Poké Ball. Pikachu prefers to hang out right on Ash's shoulder.

Don't try to pinch this Electric-type's cute red cheeks or you're bound to get zapped! Pikachu's cheeks are filled with electricity.

Ash's Pikachu is known for its incredibly powerful
Thunderbolt—an Attack where it surrounds itself with
electricity until it bursts, blasting an opponent . . . or a
bicycle. Ash met his pals Misty and May after Pikachu
fried their two-wheelers with its Thunderbolt.

Because Pikachu is so well-liked, in an effort to look less scary, Mimikyu turned some rags into a wonky Pikachu costume it wears all the time. Unfortunately, it has the opposite effect and creeps everybody out.

Although Ash and Pikachu are inseparable now, Pikachu did not like Ash at first. Without a trusty pair of rubber gloves to block its electric discharges, Ash might not have been able to handle his new pal.

In the Kalos region, a movie director named Frank runs Pikachu Manor. He cares for Cosplay Pikachu, including: Pikachu Belle, Pikachu, PhD, Pikachu Libre, Pikachu Rockstar, and Pikachu Pop Star.

After an intense battle with Lt. Surge and Raichu at the Vermillion Gym, Ash's pal Pikachu decides it never wants to evolve.

"There's more to raising a Pokémon than forcing it to evolve! And I like this Pikachu just the way it is!"
– Ash to Lt. Surge

Pikachu helped Ash win the first ever
Alola League with their Z-Move 10,000,000
Volt Thunderbolt. Kaboom!

Ash's Pikachu loves ketchup.

It puts it on everything it can and even used the bottle as a shield in a battle with Scyther.

RAICHU #026

If Raichu ever needs more energy, it can simply lift its tail toward the sky to soak in the electricity in the air.

A Raichu named Sugar loves to bake with its trainer, Abigail. No oven necessary; the secret to their unique cake flavor—Raichu's Thunderbolt.

In Galar, Pikachu flock to a special mountainside known to have Thunder Stones so they can find one and evolve into Raichu.

Raichu is two feet, seven inches tall and weighs 66.1. pounds. Its Alolan form is slightly smaller at two feet, four inches tall and weighs 46.3 pounds.

GYARADOS #130

Whatever you do, don't make Gyarados mad. When it goes on a rampage, it doesn't stop until it has burned everything to the ground with its brutal Hyper Beam. And its fire is so ferocious not even a rainstorm can stop it.

Giant Gyarados is over twenty-one feet tall and weighs more than 500 pounds, and it certainly uses its size to terrify. The Atrocious Pokémon is one aggressive Water- and Flying-type.

Lance, of the Indigo Elite Four, trains a unique red Gyarados. While helping Lance battle Team Aqua and Team Magma, Ash and his pals also found that Gyarados is an awesome way to travel, if it offers you a ride.

After a lot of taunting, James from Team Rocket abandons Magikarp. This makes it so angry it evolves into Gyarados.

JIGGLYPUFF #039

Jigglypuff evolves from Igglybuff
and can evolve into Wigglytuff.
Jigglypuff, Igglybuff, and
Wigglytuff were all reclassified
as Normal- and Fairy-types.

Jigglypuff is a singer, artist, and jokester.
It has the most beautiful, hypnotizing voice
and it likes to sing lullabies.

But when its audience falls asleep, Jigglypuff is known to scribble on their faces with a marker.

When Professor Samson Oak discovers that
Jigglypuff's song doesn't put his partner Komala
to sleep, he decides to play a prank. Komala sings
with Jigglypuff causing the pink Pokémon to pass
out. Then, Komala scribbles with a marker all over
Jigglypuff's face. When it wakes up, it finds its
temporary tattoo very funny!

The pink Balloon Pokémon has a
phenomenal lung capacity. This must help
it hold those long notes when it sings.

MEOWTH #052

The average Meowth is 1 foot, four inches tall, but when it Gigantamaxes, it grows to over 108 feet, three inches!

This Pokémon loves to collect shiny things.

If it's in a good mood, it just might let its
Trainer have a peak at its treasure hoard.

Meowth has an Alolan Form that is accustomed to luxury, having lived with Alolan royalty. Meowth's Galarian Form has lived with a savage, seafaring people which has toughed its body so much that parts of it have turned to iron!

Team Rocket's Meowth is one of the very few Pokémon who can communicate in human language, and it shows off that skill with all of the wisecracks it makes!

SLOWPOKE #079

Slowpoke is a bit oblivious and slow-witted. If its tail gets eaten, it luckily won't feel any pain, but it's unlikely to notice when it grows back either!

Slowpoke is one of the few Pokémon that fishes. It uses its tail to hook them.

Not even the top Pokémon experts can tell what Slowpoke is thinking, so it is unclear whether they even think at all. No wonder they're known as the Dopey Pokémon.

Slowpoke evolves in a very unusual way. For Slowpoke, it's not about strength, practice, or even friendship with its Trainer. When the Pokémon Shellder clamps onto its tail, then—and only then—does it become Slowbro.

Slowking's latent intelligence was drawn out when Shellder poison raced through its brain.

TOGEPI #175

Tiny Togepi is a Fairy-type Pokémon. Its evolved forms Togetic and Togekiss are Fairy- and Flying-types.

Togepi is thought to be a good luck charm. If you are sweet to the Spike Ball Pokémon, it will return the kindness by sharing its good fortune.

Togepi's shell is supposedly full of pure joy.
It's known to give its friends the warm fuzzies.

Ash found an egg. Brock and Meowth helped care
for it. But when it hatched, it bonded with Misty and
the two have been together ever since. With Misty's
friendship and dedication, it even evolved into Togetic.

EEVEE #133

Eevee's genes are so flexible that depending on where, how, and what helps it evolve, it could become eight different currently known forms—Vaporeon, Jolteon, Flareon, Espeon, Umbreon, Leafeon, Glaceon, or Sylveon.

The Battling Eevee Brothers are obsessed with evolution and their best friends Jolteon, Vaporeon, Flareon, and Eevee.

They throw a party full of local Evolution Stones to help other trainers evolve their Pokémon.

Team Eevee is a division of the Pokémon
Rescue Squad that includes Eevee and
seven of its evolutions. Their mission is to
help anyone in danger, and they also helped
their Trainer Virgil win the Unova League.

Eevee is cute, but it's also fierce. It's always ready for a friendly battle.

VAPOREON #134

Eevee evolves into Water-type Vaporeon with the help of a Water Stone.

If you need to bring an umbrella, Vaporeon will let you know. When it's going to rain, its fins jiggle.

JOLTEON #135

Eevee evolves into Electric-type Jolteon with the help of a Thunder Stone.

Jolteon absorbs negative ions from the air and turns them into a shocking 10,000-volt bolt of lightning. Zap!

Don't pet Jolteon or you might get pricked! Its fur is made of sharp needles that poke out when it's provoked.

FLAREON #136

Eevee evolves into Fire-type Flareon with the help of a Fire Stone.

Inside its flame pouch, Flareon can heat air to over 3,000 degrees Fahrenheit.

You might have to stay home if you have a fever of over 100 degrees, but it's not unusual for Flareon to have a temperature of 1,700 degrees!

ESPEON #196

Eevee evolves into Psychic-type Espeon in the sunshine.

Espeon has a special sensitivity to air currents that gives it incredibly valuable insights. It can sense its foe's next move and even predict the weather.

Between Espeon's eyes lies a shiny orb from which it fires its psychic power. If the orb is dark, Espeon needs to recharge its energy.

UMBREON #197

Eevee evolves into Dark-type Umbreon while bathed in moonlight.

You might not need a flashlight to find Umbreon at night—the golden rings on its body glow when there's a full moon or if it's excited.

Umbreon can get so fired up with anger that it sweats poison. Then, it sprays the foul toxin into its foe's eyes.

LEAFEON #470

Eevee evolves into Grass-type Leafeon with the help of a Moss Rock.

Leafeon's cells are so similar to a plant's that it can create its own energy with photosynthesis. Its tail is so sharp it can slice through thick tree trunks.

Leafeon's leaves create a distinctive aroma favored by Galarians. There's even a popular perfume that uses that scent.

GLACEON #471

Eevee evolves into Ice-type Glaceon with the help of an Ice Rock.

Glaceon gives off a frosty chill that turns into powdery snow. However, anyone who becomes captivated by the snowfall's beauty will be frozen before they know it!

Glaceon's gorgeous snow has been known to put on quite a show. But if you watch it fall for too long, you'll become frozen like an ice cube.

SYLVEON #700

Eevee can evolve into Fairy-type Sylveon when it feels truly loved by its Trainer and has the ability to perform at least one Fairy-type move.

Sylveon is the ultimate peacemaker. With a wave of its ribbonlike feelers, it can release any anger and end any conflict.

Sylveon prefers peace, but it will fight for what is right. According to a Galarian fairy tale, sweet Sylveon stepped up to defeat a nasty dragon Pokémon.

BULBASAUR #001

If you're a lucky Trainer beginning your journey in Kanto, you can ask Professor Oak to have Bulbasaur be your First Partner Pokémon.

Grass- and Poison-type Bulbasaur is born with a seed on its back. It is full of nutrients to help it grow.

Bulbasaur gather together to evolve.
Flowers and a giant, ancient tree burst into
bloom for the beautiful secret ceremony in
the Mysterious Garden.

IVYSAUR #002

Ivysaur is the evolved form of Bulbasaur. The key to keeping it strong is lots of sunshine.

The bulb on its back can grow so big that Ivysaur looks as though it cannot stand on its hind legs anymore.

Ivysaur used to gather in a special spot in Vermilion City to sunbathe, but the site has since been turned into a gym.

VENUSAUR #003

Like its pre-evolved forms Bulbasaur and Ivysaur, Venusaur loves to soak up the sun. When it feels those rays on its back, its flower blooms.

Amazingly enough, Venusaur can Mega Evolve and Gigantamax. Venusaur is six foot, seven inches tall. Mega Venusaur grows to seven foot, ten inches tall and Gigantamax Venusaur can be over seventy-eight feet, nine inches tall!

During the exhibition battle of the first Alola League, Ash battled his mentor Professor Kukui. One of the coolest moments was when the Professor's pal Venusaur trapped Ash's Rowlet in its flower!

SQUIRTLE #007

If you're a new Trainer in the Kanto Region, you might get to choose the Tiny Turtle Pokémon as your First Partner Pokémon.

Squirtle has a hard shell it can hide in if a foe tries to attack. But if it only pulls its neck in, that means it's going to fire a blast of water. Look out!

It can also aim and shoot streams of water at any target. Because of this skill, Squirtle are known to be excellent firefighters and even hold a firefighting competition.

The Squirtle Squad is a gang of Squirtle that hang out in Kanto region. Their leader wears an awesome pair of sunglasses. It traveled around with Ash for a while before returning to the squad.

WARTORTLE #008

The evolved form of Squirtle is Wartortle. You can guess Wartortle's age from the shell on its back. If it's covered in algae, it's old.

Wartortle's ears are covered in hair. The furry features help it stay steady when it swims.

At the Wallace Cup, Pokémon Coordinator May and Wartortle wowed fans with an Aqua Tail that sprayed water all over the stadium.

BLASTOISE #009

From its two water cannons, Blastoise can fire blasts so strong that a fire hose looks like a trickle.

At five feet, three inches, Blastoise is already quite big and stays the exact same height when it Mega Evolves. However, when it Gigantamaxes, it grows to over eighty-two feet tall.

Blastoise might be a big dude, but it's light on its feet. Trainer Tierno and Blastoise have a special strategy where they dance together to the beat of the battle.

CHARMANDER #004

Fire-type Charmander is so hot that its tail turns rain into steam.

New Trainers in the Kanto Region can choose fiery Charmander to be their First Partner Pokémon. It is known as the Lizard Pokémon.

Charmander has a flame on its tail that burns from birth. Worry if it ever gets weak and take Charmander to see Nurse Joy right away! That's precisely what Ash did when he saw a sad, abandoned Charmander sitting in the rain, and they've been friends ever since.

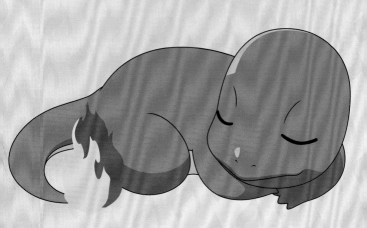

CHARMELEON #005

Brutal Charmeleon does not hold back in battle! It whacks foes with its flaming tail and strikes with its super sharp claws.

When Charmeleon gets really angry, especially in a heated battle, it will shoot fierce flames to burn everything down to ash.

Sunburst Island is known for its local artists that make gorgeous glass crafts. Charmeleon's Fire-type Attacks are so intense it helps artist Mateo shape his glass sculptures.

CHARIZARD #006

For thousands of years, Charicific Valley has been a wild Charizard habitat where tourists are not welcome. Even every Charizard must compete to prove it's strong enough to be worthy of this sanctuary.

Charizard can breathe out a flame so fierce it will reduce a boulder to dust

Charizard can fly about 4,600 feet up in the sky. It has also been known to offer its Trainer a ride.

Charizard can Mega Evolve
into Charizard X or Charizard Y.
It can also Gigantamax!

INSIGHT
EDITIONS

PO Box 3088
San Rafael, CA 94912
www.insighteditions.com

Find us on Facebook: www.facebook.com/InsightEditions

Follow us on Twitter: @insighteditions

Published by Insight Editions, San Rafael, California, in 2021.

Library of Congress Cataloging-in-Publication Data available.

ISBN: 978-1-64722-672-5

Publisher: Raoul Goff
VP of Licensing and Partnerships:
Vanessa Lopez
VP of Creative: Chrissy Kwasnik
VP of Manufacturing: Alix Nicholaeff
VP, Editorial Director: Vicki Jaeger
Senior Designer: Monique Narboneta Zosa

Senior Editor: Jennifer Sims
Assistant Editor: Harrison Tunggal
Associate Editor: Sadie Lowry
Senior Production Editor: Elaine Ou
Senior Production Manager: Greg Steffen
Senior Production Manager, Subsidiary
Rights: Lina s Palma-Temena

Text by Simcha Whitehill

ROOTS of PEACE   REPLANTED PAPER

Insight Editions, in association with Roots of Peace, will plant two trees for each tree used in the manufacturing of this book. Roots
of Peace is an internationally renowned humanitarian organization dedicated to eradicating land mines worldwide and converting
war-torn lands into productive farms.

Manufactured in China by Insight Editions.

10 9 8 7 6 5 4 3 2